Series 401
A Ladybird Book

THE FIRST DAY OF THE HOLIDAYS.
The adventures of penguins Pen and Gwen,
who preferred mischief to the task of shelling
peas for Mother Penguin, will delight all
young children.

THE FIRST DAY OF THE HOLIDAYS

Story and illustrations by
A. J. MACGREGOR

Verses by
W. PERRING

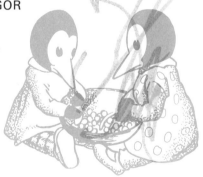

Ladybird Books Loughborough

Summer holidays had started:

    Pen and Gwen were sleeping late.

Mother Penguin came and called them,

    " Hurry! Breakfast cannot wait!"

Little penguins, dressing quickly,

    Scattered garments left and right,

Dropping odds and ends around them,

    Till the bedroom was a sight !

Down the stairs they tiptoed softly,

    Father frowned with watch in hand:

"You are late again for breakfast,

    Hurry!" was his stern command.

"We are very sorry, Father,

Please forgive us both!" said Gwen.

Down they sat, and gobbled breakfast:

"I *am* hungry!" mumbled Pen.

Soon there was an empty table :

    Then to Father's chair they ran.

Pen said " Picnic ! ", Gwen said " Fishing ! "

    What a chatter now began.

But the chatter soon was ended !

Mrs. Pen was at the door,

Holding baskets for the children !

. . . What were empty baskets for ?

" First, my dears, you'll fill these baskets

    Full of peas for us to eat ! "

How the sulky pair of penguins

    Wept and sobbed and stamped their feet !

Father Penguin said " No nonsense !

Go and get your baskets full ! "

Sadly then they sought the garden :

How they wished they were at school !

Doleful penguins in the garden

    Thought of what they might have done;

Filling baskets full of pea-pods

    Wasn't their idea of fun!

Suddenly they heard a scratching:

Pen turned round and gave a shout;

In the basket was a blackbird,

Pecking all the peas about!

Off the cheeky robber fluttered,

    With a pea-pod in his beak;

Pen jumped high and flapped his flippers,

    Almost too annoyed to speak!

Pen, alas! was not a flier,

    Down he came, a nasty smack:

Mrs. Penguin heard the noises,

    Called, "It's time that you were back!"

Pen was angrier than ever ;

    " Ow ! I've hurt my foot ! " he cried.

Gwen said " Let me make a bandage ! "

    Soon the foot was neatly tied !

Then came Mrs. Penguin to them:

Saw they hadn't many peas;

Said, " I've brought a bowl for shelling:

You must gather more than these!"

Down sat Gwen, without a murmur,

With the bowl upon her knee :

"What, and shell them?" Pen exploded,

"This is far too much for me!"

Off he darted, through the pea-sticks,

Saying, " I am going out! "

Gwen was nervous, tried to stop him:

Suddenly he gave a shout!

Crawling through the thorns and branches,

Pen had come into the lane,

Saw the shining motor-cycle,

"Come on, Gwen!" he called again.

Then he looked all round the cycle,

    Clean and gleaming in the sun;

Played about with knobs and levers,

    Thought, "A joy-ride *would* be fun!"

Now came Gwen: and Pen, excited,

Said, "This *is* a lucky find!"

Then he clambered on the saddle;

Gwen, uncertain, climbed behind.

Pen said, "What about a joy-ride?"

    "I can't drive," said Gwen, "Can you?"

"Why, of course!" Pen answered boldly,

    Pulled some knob . . . and off they flew!

Flashing by the trees and hedges:

"Stop!" wailed Gwen: "I wish I
could!"

Pen replied: for, in the roadway,

Flapping hard, the owner stood!

But the swerving, speeding cycle,

    With its naughty penguin load,

Quickly stopped his angry flapping,

    Knocked him backwards on the road !

Pen and Gwen were sadly frightened,

    Though they were not hurt at all :

But the raging owner shook them ;

    He had not enjoyed his fall.

Then came Mrs. Penguin to him,
    Said how sorry were the pair:
So the owner quite forgave them,
    Left them to their Mother's care!

. . . Mother's care! But Mrs. Penguin
    Proved a mother hard to please!
Pen and Gwen were soundly scolded,
    Then sent back to . . . pick the peas!